P9-DNP-068

In keeping with Islamic tradition, the makers of this book have decided not to depict the Prophet Muhammad.

For Akash, Lilla and Calin.
And in memory of David Bolduc. — GO

For my friend Soheil. — LW

Published in Canada and the USA in 2013 by Groundwood Books

Groundwood Books / House of Anansi Press
110 Spadina Avenue, Suite 801, Toronto, Ontario M5V 2K4
or c/o Publishers Group West
1700 Fourth Street, Berkeley, CA 94710

We acknowledge for their financial support of our publishing program the Canada Council for the Arts, the Government of Canada through the Canada Book Fund (CBF) and the Ontario Arts Council.

Canada Council for the Arts
Conseil des Arts du Canada

Library and Archives Canada Cataloguing in Publication
Ondaatje, Griffin
The camel in the sun / written by Griffin Ondaatje ; illustrated by Linda Wolfsgruber.
ISBN 978-1-55498-381-0
1. Animals in the Hadith — Juvenile literature. 2. Islamic stories.
I. Wolfsgruber, Linda II. Title.
BP135.8.A54054 2013 j297.1'2512 C2013-900377-0

The illustrations are monoprints with drawing.
Design by Michael Solomon
Printed and bound in Malaysia

The Camel in the Sun

BY

Griffin Ondaatje

PICTURES BY

Linda Wolfsgruber

GROUNDWOOD BOOKS
HOUSE OF ANANSI PRESS
TORONTO BERKELEY

In the lands east of the Red Sea, past the mountains of Hejaz, there was a camel. It had worked all its life for a merchant, Halim, carrying goods back and forth across the desert. It often walked all the way from Al-Hasa oasis to the sea at Jeddah.

The old camel carried large bundles filled with spices, dates, incense, silk, silver and wool. Before each journey, its owner would make it kneel so he could climb on its back and settle on top of all the bundles. Then the camel would stand and start to walk.

The camel climbed the steep sand dunes and walked along the tops of them and then lumbered down their other side, almost tumbling over and spilling everything. On the flat stretches of the desert, when nightfall was approaching, the man always yelled at the camel to run, so he could reach the place where he'd sell his goods as fast as possible.

They rarely stopped to rest. The camel's whole life was spent struggling across the oceans of sand. By the time it arrived at their destination, it would stand breathing in and out noisily, with foam gathering around its mouth. Then it would wait patiently in the sun while its owner climbed down and walked over to the shade to sit and talk business with other merchants.

One day, suddenly, after years of walking in the burning sun over the desert's sandy waves, the camel felt water rising in its eyes.

At first it didn't know what was happening. The camel thought perhaps its eyes were hurting from the winds blowing sand in its face. But it was tears that were filling its eyes. The camel stood still and breathed out a long sigh.

The owner climbed off its back and stared at the camel. When he saw that the camel was just tired and sad, he said, "The slower you walk … the longer till you drink water." And he climbed up again.

The old camel never showed its sadness to Halim again. In the evening, though, when Halim had fallen asleep among the bundles, the camel sighed under the huge night sky. It walked along, dragging its nose-string across the sand, biting its lip and looking up at the stars. It was lonely now, as it thought that there was no one it could tell about its long life of suffering and hard work.

And so for the next few months the camel continued walking in the hot sun. But at night it drifted away like a boat, often with the bundles still tied to its back, and sank behind a sand dune and sighed to itself until morning.

As for Halim, he would sleep soundly, and during the day he'd ride on the camel's back as if he were floating over the desert on a bundle of valuable goods under which there was no camel.

One day they approached the outskirts of Medina. Medina was a beautiful city with a hundred gardens, and it was said that the Prophet lived there. The merchant was looking forward to resting there before traveling on south to Najran.

They passed through the narrow city gate and entered a garden where some people were gathered in the shade of tall palm trees. Halim tied the camel to a post in the blazing sun. Then he walked over to the shade and sat down.

He drank water, ate some dates and talked business with the other merchants. When he was done, he piled up a pillow of sand and lay down and fell asleep in the shade.

The camel stood still, alone, with the bundles on its back. A few hours passed. It stood patiently in the hot sun.

The Prophet, who was indeed living in Medina, was out for a walk that afternoon, and he entered the garden. He looked over and saw the merchant resting in the shade of the trees,

and then he turned and saw the camel standing
in the hot sun. He saw how the camel was tied to
a post, barely able to stand, looking sad.

The Prophet crossed into the bright sunlight and walked straight up and hugged the camel's neck, pressing his face against its long bony face. He stared into the camel's surprised black eyes and then offered his shoulder for support.

The camel leaned heavily on the Prophet's shoulder and burst into tears. It heaved with long sobs of unhappiness. Its whole body shook — the way animals shake when they cry in secret.

And then something happened. The tears falling from the camel's eyes fell on the sand and sank down, and somehow they sifted into Halim's dream. And soon Halim began to see through the camel's eyes.

Dreaming there in the cool shade, Halim felt his heart ache with sadness. He saw for the first time how hot and tired the camel was, and he felt, as the camel felt, that he had led a lifetime of pain and loneliness. He lay there and wept in his dream, into his pillow of sand, while the camel cried against the shoulder of the Prophet.

When the camel had finally finished crying, the Prophet stood back and looked over at the sleeping man who was still crying.

"Are you the camel's owner?" he asked.

"Messenger of God, I ..." answered the man from where he lay still half-asleep under the tree. He was about to speak when a wave of sadness came over him again, and he lost his voice and was unable to say anything else.

"Can't you see that the camel is sad?" said the Prophet.

The man could find no words. Finally, the Prophet turned and slowly walked away.

Halim felt his face grow hotter and hotter. He was feverish. He felt as though the sun's flames, as sharp as pineapple leaves, were falling onto his face.

He sat up. He saw the camel staring after the Prophet.

Halim could still feel tears on his face. He walked over and untied the camel, then reached up and stroked its neck and stood quietly beside it. Then he gave the camel water and guided it gently into the shade of the trees.

"We will rest a while before we go on ..." he said softly. "There is no need to hurry."

AUTHOR'S NOTE

PART OF THE INSPIRATION for this book was a brief story told to me in 1994, while I was visiting family in Sri Lanka. At that time I was researching a collection of Buddhist, Hindu and Muslim stories, and heard a retelling from a Muslim man from Colombo. He told several stories relating to compassion — ones he'd known since childhood. His brief account of a tired camel, its hardhearted owner and their life-changing encounter with the Prophet stayed with me. Some stories of compassion feel instantly familiar. Perhaps, in some ways, the camel standing quietly in the sun stands close to all of us. For me, its suffering carried the silent heart of the story.

A few years ago, for various reasons, I revisited the story and began to write *The Camel in the Sun*. When I first heard it, I didn't know that the story came from a *hadith* — an account of the Prophet's words or actions passed from generation to generation. It was while reading a booklet entitled *Animal Welfare in Islamic Law* that I recognized the storyline in a translation attributed to Abu Dawud's collection of hadith. It described a similar encounter in a garden: the Prophet discovers an overworked and starving camel and immediately instructs its owner to care for it properly. The message was direct and clear. How the Prophet dealt so openly and compassionately with the situation — first comforting the suffering animal and then enlightening the owner — remained powerful and unforgettable. The camel's owner is compelled to change and suddenly faces a crucial moment in his life. Perhaps he is like most of us who have — somewhere in life — left a camel in the sun, whatever that "camel" may be ... maybe it is even part of ourselves.

The story of the camel, at least in part, carries a significant narrative to some readers. Today there are, of course, many retellings and translations available of numerous hadith (in historical and academic books, religious texts, books for children, and hadith sites online). Words of a specific hadith may vary between translations, and various hadith may be similar. This book is not in any way a translation, or a complete retelling. It is intended simply as a respectful and imagined story, inspired by a hadith. A range of retellings of hadith (in their entirety or in part) can be found in formats suitable for diverse audiences of all ages; popular children's books such as Saniyasnain Khan's *Goodnight Stories from the Life of the Prophet Muhammad*, for instance, are now widely read and translated.

ACKNOWLEDGMENTS

First I'd like to give my thanks and love to Sang-Mi, and to the rest of my family. I also want to thank Patsy Aldana, my great editor, who supported and believed in the book and helped shape it from the beginning. Linda Wolfsgruber's illustrations are beautiful and luminous, and I'm very grateful to share the same page. Thanks to Nan Froman, Michael Solomon, Sheila Barry and everyone at Groundwood. Thanks also to the wonderfully generous scholars, Professor Walid Saleh at the University of Toronto, and Professor Kristen A. Stilt at Northwestern University in Chicago. Both kindly read the story and gave helpful and thoughtful insights and encouragement. The following works were also helpful as resources: *Animal Welfare in Islam* by Al-Hafiz B.A. Masri; *Animal Welfare in Islamic Law* by Kristen A. Stilt; *Animals in Islamic Tradition and Muslim Cultures* by Richard C. Foltz; *Hadith: Muhammad's Legacy in the Medieval and Modern World* by Jonathan A.C. Brown; and *Muhammad: Man and Prophet* by Adil Salahi.

— GO

January 2013